The animals were sitting in their usual spot waiting for a bedtime story when...

PREPOSTEROUS RHINOCEROS

by Tracy Gunaratnam

Illustrated by Marta Costa

"Disaster!" shrieked Drama Llama. "King Lion has lost his voice! There will be NO bedtime stories until he finds it!"

"Shy Salamander can read," snapped Cranky Crocodile.

"She's shy and she doesn't want to," said Rhinoceros. "But luckily, I do!"

"That's PREPOSTEROUS, Rhinoceros!" the crowd cried.

"You don't know anything about books."

"I know that the king can tell a story when he opens one," said Rhinoceros.

The animals were too tired to argue.

"All right," they said.

Rhinoceros turned to the first page... and waited.

He waited and waited and waited... NOTHING happened.

Then he took a key from his pocket. Perhaps if
I wind it up, he thought, but that didn't help!

So he shook it!

He shook it and shook it until the pages fell out!

The animals groaned. There would be no bedtime story tonight.

The next morning Rhinoceros declared,
"I need some storytelling advice!"

And off he charged, deep into the jungle.

"Hello Drama Llama," said Rhinoceros, "Do you know
how to use a book?"

"Just open it and dive straight in," Drama Llama replied.

Rhinoceros placed the book at the bottom of the tallest rock in the jungle, and he began to climb, up, up, up, all the way to the very top.

Then he snapped on his goggles, stood on his tippy toes and...

dived head first into the book, "Weeeeeeee..."

SMASH!

"That's preposterous, Rhinoceros!" said Shy Salamander.

"I need some PROPER storytelling advice!" declared Rhinoceros, and he charged deeper into the jungle.

"Excuse me, Techie Toucan," said Rhinoceros, "do you know how to use a book?"

"Just open it and get stuck in," Techie Toucan replied.

So Rhinoceros smothered himself in sticky honey, and got stuck in.

"That's preposterous, Rhinoceros!" sighed Shy Salamander.

The jungle animals laughed their socks off.

"It's not funny!" said Rhinoceros.

Shy Salamander tried everything to get her friend's attention but it was no use until...

"RHINO

"Books don't need keys, tall rocks or sticky honey!
They just need to be READ!"

Rhinoceros looked up. "RED!" he said,

"Why didn't you say so?"

"Not that sort of red," said Shy Salamander,
"Come on, I'll show you."

Learning to read was sometimes tricky
but so much fun and eventually...

Rhinoceros was ready to read the bedtime story.
He opened the book and...

RRROOOOA

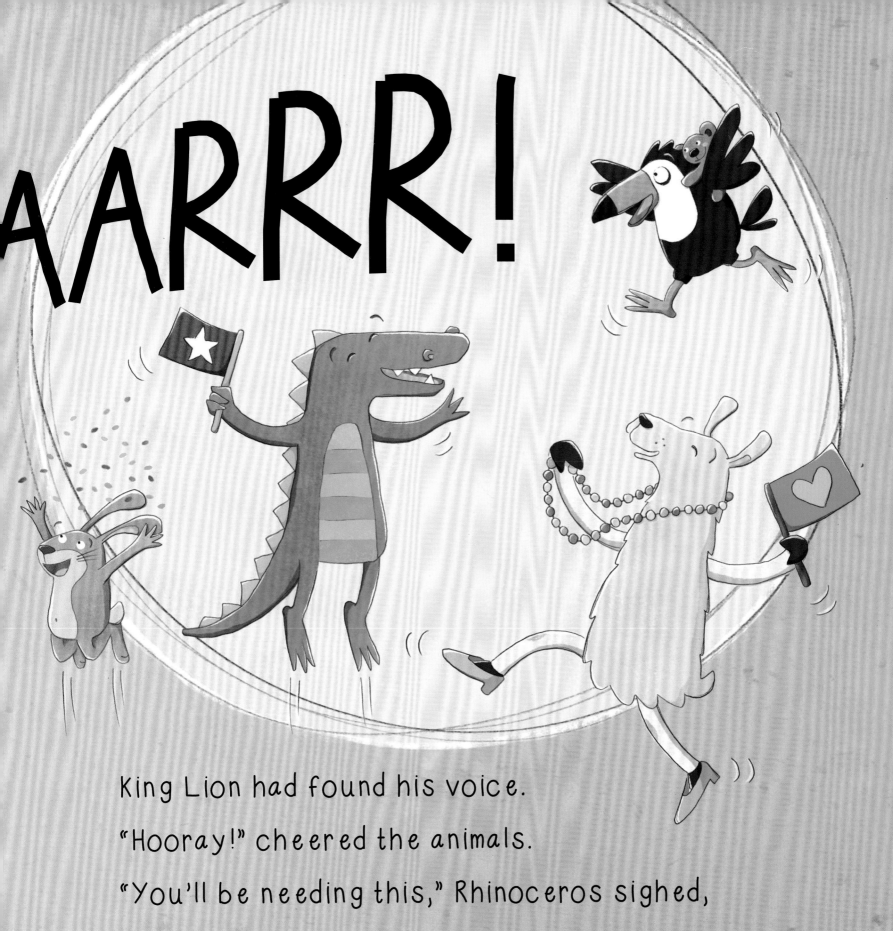

King Lion had found his voice.

"Hooray!" cheered the animals.

"You'll be needing this," Rhinoceros sighed,

handing him the book.

"Not so fast!" said King Lion.
"I think it's time someone read ME
a bedtime story for a change!"

Rhinoceros beamed with pride as he sat down and
read his favourite story right to **the end.**

Preposterous Rhinoceros

is an original concept by

© Tracy Gunaratnam

Illustrator: Marta Costa

Represented by Plum Pudding

Published by MAVERICK ARTS PUBLISHING LTD

Studio 3A, City Business Centre, 6 Brighton Road,

Horsham, West Sussex, RH13 5BB

© Maverick Arts Publishing Limited January 2015 +44 (0)1403 256941

A CIP catalogue record for this book is available at the British Library.

ISBN 978-1-84886-165-7

www.maverickbooks.co.uk